MW00962715

GREAT JOURNEYS

Peter Chrisp

RSVP

RAINTREE
STECK-VAUGHN
P U B L I S H E R S
The Steck-Vaughn Company

Austin, Texas

THE REMARKABLE WORLD

Published by Raintree Steck-Vaughn Publishers, an imprint of Steck-Vaughn Company

Library of Congress Cataloging-in-Publication Data
Chrisp, Peter.
Great journeys / Peter Chrisp.
    p.   cm.—(Remarkable world)
Includes bibliographical references (p. -) and index.
Summary: An account of explorers and their journeys including those along the rivers of North America, across the deserts of Australia, and to the region around the South Pole.
ISBN 0-8172-4537-5
1. Discoveries in geography—Juvenile literature.
[1. Discoveries in geography. 2. Explorers.]
I. Title. II. Series.
G175.C465   1996
910'.9—dc20   95-43277

Printed in Italy and bound in the United States
1 2 3 4 5 6 7 8 9 0 01 00 99 98 97

Photo acknowledgments
AKG, London 8t; Bruce Coleman Ltd. 36–37; ET Archive *front cover (middle left), front cover (bottom left)*, 4, 6, 7, 11, 12, 13, 20, 23, 25t, 27b, 44–45; Mary Evans Picture Library *title page*, 8b, 10–11, 18, 22 both, 24, 27t, 28t, 31t, 34, 35, 37, 38b, 39 both, 41, 42; Image Select 28b, 33, 38t; Peter Newark's Pictures *front cover (right)*, 5, 10t, 10b, 14, 15 both, 16–17, 17, 18–19, 19, 21, 25b, 29t, 30 both, 31b, 43b; Photri 9, 40, 43t; Trip 4b; Wayland Picture Library *front cover (top)*, 14b, 29b. The artwork is by Peter Bull 6, 9, 12, 16, 19, 24, 26, 28, 32b, 44; and Tony Townsend 32t, 41.

CONTENTS

TRAVELERS' TALES

Below Many early Chinese travelers, including Hsüan-tsang, were Buddhists who went to central and southern Asia in search of religious knowledge. Others followed the silk routes, carrying silks, spices, and gems to the Middle East and Europe.

Inset Hsüan-tsang

"Alone and abandoned, he crossed the sandy waste, with no means of finding the way except by following the heaps of bones and horse dung…. The view was endless…and in the night the demons and goblins raised firelights as many as the stars; in the daytime, the wind blew the sand before it."

It was the year A.D. 629, and a Chinese monk named Hsüan-tsang was traveling west, across the Gobi Desert. He was on his way to India. This land was the birthplace of his religion, Buddhism, and he hoped to study the Buddhist teachings at their source.

We know about Hsüan-tsang's journey thanks to his book, *The Record of the Western Regions*. It is full of details of the dangers of travel: "The roads were very dangerous and the valleys gloomy. Sometimes one had to cross on rope bridges, sometimes by clinging to chains. Now there were gangways hanging in midair, now flying bridges flung across precipices."

After reaching India, Hsüan-tsang went from monastery to monastery, studying the sacred

Buddha preaches to his followers in this thousand-year-old banner from China. Hundreds of years before this, Buddhists had begun traveling from China to India to study their religion at its source.

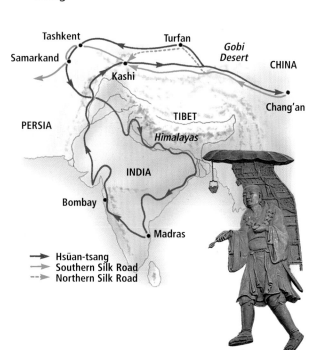

Tashkent
Samarkand
Turfan
Gobi Desert
CHINA
Kashi
Chang'an
TIBET
PERSIA
Himalayas
INDIA
Bombay
Madras

→ Hsüan-tsang
→ Southern Silk Road
--→ Northern Silk Road

Who were the first explorers?

The earliest explorers of the world left no books, and so we know almost nothing about them. Some 50,000 years ago, people from Asia crossed the sea to Australia. Later, perhaps 30,000 years ago, other people walked across a bridge of land from Asia to North America. Who were these people? Why did they set off on their great journeys? We will never know, for their names and their stories are now lost forever.

books and questioning holy men. Then he set off on the long journey home. In A.D. 645, after sixteen years away, he came back to his own monastery. He had brought with him a priceless cargo of over 650 Buddhist texts.

Hsüan-tsang was one of many Chinese monks who made the difficult journey to India. He is the most famous of them because his book, *The Record of the Western Regions* still exists.

A mission to the Mongols

Between 1213 and 1260, the Mongols, a fierce people from Central Asia, conquered the biggest land empire that has ever existed. It stretched from southern Russia all the way to the Pacific Ocean. They also invaded eastern Europe in 1241, turning back only because of the death of their ruler, Ögödei Khan.

Fierce Mongol warriors attack a Chinese town in 1205. The Mongols were held in terror by much of the civilized world during the thirteenth century and were credited with building small hills from the skulls of their enemies.

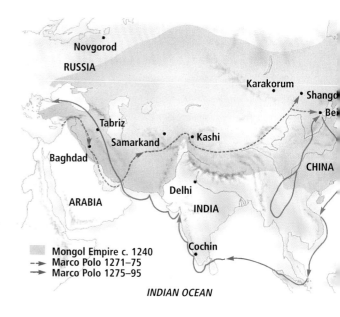

Few explorers embarked on their travels simply to gain knowledge of other lands. Most—including Marco Polo, shown here with his camel cara-van—went because they hoped to get rich through trade.

The Pope, the head of the Catholic Church in Western Europe, wanted to find out who the invaders were and what they planned to do next. He sent a mission to the Mongol court. It was led by a very unlikely traveler, Friar Giovanni de Pian del Carpini. When he set off, in April 1246, he was 65 years old and was so fat that he had trouble walking.

Friar Giovanni journeyed by day and night, with horses and protection from the Mongols. As he passed through Asia, he saw many signs of the recent conquests: "We found many skulls and bones of dead men lying upon the ground like cattle dung… we found innumerable cities with ruined castles, and many towns left desolate."

After traveling almost three thousand miles, he arrived at the Mongol court just in time to see the coronation of the new khan, Güyük. This khan gave him a message to give to the Pope: "Today you shall say from the depths of your heart: we wish to be Your subjects… You

At its height, the Mongol Empire covered a vast area of Asia and part of Eastern Europe. It took Marco Polo, his father, and his uncle three and a half years to travel from Venice to Shangdu, Kublai Khan's summer capital. Their journey started from the eastern end of the Mediterranean Sea, shown on the left of this map.

6

must therefore come to Us on behalf of all kings, and offer your services… If you ignore Our wishes, we shall consider you as Our enemies."

Luckily for the Pope, the Mongols did not return to invade Europe.

Following the Silk Road

After 106 B.C., the riches of the far east, such as silk, porcelain, and metalware from China, traveled west on camel caravans along a route known as the Silk Road. These were brought by Chinese, Persian, Arab, and Jewish merchants. It was a long and dangerous journey, and the travelers crossed deserts and lands infested by bandits.

Under Mongol rule, travel along the Silk Road became much safer. The whole route was ruled by a single people for the first time, and the Mongols encouraged trade. Taking advantage of the "Mongol Peace," some European traders began to travel east along the Silk Road.

Marco Polo leaves the harbor of Venice on his way to the East. Polo stayed away from home for 24 years, then returned with tales of his travels so fantastic that few people believed them.

Marco Polo

The most famous of all European travelers was a Venetian merchant, Marco Polo (1254–1324). In 1260, his father and uncle had made their first trip along the Silk Road to China and were welcomed by the last great Mongol khan, Kublai.

A Muslim caravan on its way to Mecca

When they returned to China in 1271, they took the young Marco with them.

Marco Polo spent seventeen years in the east and described what he saw in a book published in 1301. He was overwhelmed by the wealth in the palace of the Mongol leader Kublai Khan, where the walls were "covered with gold and silver and decorated with pictures of dragons and birds and horsemen."

Marco Polo's readers were certain that he was exaggerating. Some of his stories seemed simply impossible:

Ibn Battuta, the great Muslim traveler, spent 24 years on the road. Here he is visiting an Egyptian temple.

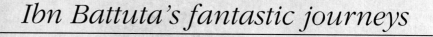

Ibn Battuta's fantastic journeys

The greatest travelers of the Middle Ages were the Muslims. Many of them visited the holy city of Mecca in modern Saudi Arabia, the birthplace of the prophet Muhammad. This pilgrimage brought people together from all the Muslim lands, which stretched from Spain to Indonesia. As a result, Muslims had a much clearer idea of the wider world than Christians.

Ibn Battuta, from Tangiers in Morocco, was a pilgrim who enjoyed traveling so much that he never stopped. Between 1325 and 1354, he visited Sardinia, Spain, West Africa, East Africa, and most of the countries of Asia. He covered 75,000 miles, making an effort never to use the same road twice. Ibn Battuta has been called the greatest traveler of all time.

"Let me tell you next of stones that burn like logs. It is a fact that throughout the province of Cathay (China) there is a sort of black stone, which is dug out of veins in the hillsides, and burns like logs. These stones keep the fire going better than wood." People who had never heard of coal found it difficult to believe this description of burning stones.

Between 1325 and 1354, Ibn Battuta traveled more than 75,000 miles through North Africa, the Middle East, and southern Europe. He often took routes that were used by Arab traders in the area of the Mediterranean Sea.

No need to explore

After the early Buddhist monks, there were few Chinese explorers. The Chinese were not usually interested in foreign lands, because they believed that other countries had nothing new to offer them.

In contrast, the Europeans knew that they were poor and that Asia was rich. The products of the east were sold at high prices in the markets of Venice. They had books of travelers' tales full of descriptions of wonders and riches. It was the search for these riches that would make the Europeans the greatest explorers of all.

The Great Wall of China guards the country against people and ideas from outside. This is the land where Marco Polo saw "stones that burn like logs"—or coal— which no one at home would believe.

Granada
Salé
Marrakesh
Fez
Tuat
Cagliari
Tunis
Tripoli
Alexandria
Jerusalem
Cairo
Taghaza
Ghat
Medina
Sahara Desert
Gao
Kawar
Mecca
Jeddah
Djenné
Koukia
Kanem
Mali
Aden
Niari
Timbuktu
Kano
Bito
AFRICA
Mogadishu
1325–27
1327–30
1330–49
1349–54
Mombasa
Kilwa

9

SEARCHING FOR KINGDOMS OF GOLD

The search for the wealth of Asia sent the Europeans west across the Atlantic Ocean. At the time, they had no idea that their route would be blocked by two vast continents, later called North and South America.

In 1492, Spanish ships under Christopher Columbus sailed west to the Americas. Columbus was certain that he had found the Indies, which Europeans called Asia, and so he called the local people "Indians."

The carved head of an Aztec warrior, a Knight of the Order of Eagles. The figure was made sometime in the fifteenth century, just before the fall of the Aztec Empire.

The conquistadors arrive

The Spaniards called themselves conquistadors (conquerors). Their horses, guns, and swords gave them a big advantage over the native peoples. The Native Americans also had no defense against diseases brought from Europe, such as smallpox and measles. One Spaniard wrote: "The Indians die so easily that the bare look and smell of a Spaniard causes them to give up the ghost."

The conquerors were convinced that they had the right to take over the Native American lands. Despite all

Hernán Cortés, the Spanish conquistador whose 508 soldiers, 100 sailors, and 16 horses overthrew the great Aztec Empire.

their violence, they thought they were doing the native people a favor by bringing them Christianity.

Between 1519 and 1535 the Spaniards conquered two great empires in America—the Aztec Empire of Mexico and the Inca Empire of Peru. Each had beautiful cities and was rich in gold and silver. These early conquests led to more journeys of exploration.

The search for the Golden King

In the 1500s, the Spaniards in South America heard many rumors of a ruler nicknamed El Dorado, or "The Golden One." He was said to be coated in gold dust every morning. He was then rowed to the middle of a lake where he washed and made offerings of gold to his gods.

Francisco Pizarro (half brother of Gonzalo) and his men, having gotten inside the Inca town of Cuzco, set about massacring the inhabitants.

In 1541, a Spaniard named Gonzalo Pizarro set off to seek the lake of El Dorado. Pizarro took with him 220 mounted Spaniards and 4,000 Native Americans. He also had thousands of dogs and pigs. The expedition went badly almost as soon as it set out. In the cold, high Andes Mountains, the Native Americans began to freeze to death. Down in the steamy jungles, pouring rain

A gold model of a king on his raft, from South America. It was treasures such as this that encouraged Pizarro to go in search of El Dorado, the golden ruler. In the end he and his men were rewarded only with death and disease.

rotted the Spaniards' shirts. Then the food ran out. The dogs and pigs had been eaten or had run away. The Spaniards began to eat their horses, while the Native Americans starved. When the rain turned the ground into a swamp, Pizarro decided to take to the Coca River. He built a small ship and sent one of his officers, Francisco de Orellana, ahead in it to find food. Pizarro never saw Orellana again.

Pizarro set off back to Quito, his men now eating their saddles and stirrup leathers. Only half of them got back home. Their return was described by an eyewitness, Agustin de Zarate: "They were traveling almost naked, for their clothes had rotted long ago with the continuous rains…. Their swords were sheathless and eaten with rust. They were all on foot, and their arms and legs were scored with wounds from the thorns and bushes…. They were almost unrecognizable."

What had happened to Orellana?

Orellana's ship had been swept downstream by the currents. It was the beginning of an eight-

In January 1531, Francisco Pizarro set out from Panama to conquer Peru. The Inca capital, Cajamarca, was captured in November 1532. The following year he captured Cuzco, the main southern Inca city. In 1541, Francisco's brother, Gonzalo, attempted to find the fabled El Dorado. He failed, but some members of the expedition, led by Francisco de Orellana, sailed down the Amazon River to the sea.

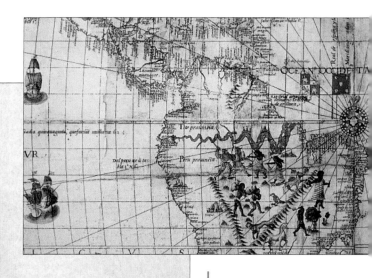

Orellana and the Amazons

One result of Orellana's journey was a new myth. He claimed to have found a tribe of fighting women. Carvajal wrote: "We ourselves saw these women, who were fighting in front of all the Indian men as women captains, and they fought so courageously that the Indian men did not dare turn their backs."

This was the part of the journey that most impressed other Europeans. The river came to be known as the River of the Amazons, after the women warriors in ancient Greek legends.

This detail from a map of the world, drawn in 1544, shows conquistadors being attacked by fearsome warrior women, who came to be called Amazons.

month voyage that would take him three thousand miles down the world's largest river, the Amazon. Gaspar de Carvajal, one of Orellana's men, described the journey: "We saw the villages glimmering white, and we had not proceeded far when we saw coming up the river a great many canoes, all equipped for fighting, gaily colored.... They were coming on with great yells, playing on many drums and wooden trumpets, threatening us as if they were going to eat us."

The Spaniards had to fight many battles, and Orellana lost an eye to an arrow. They also spent many boring days drifting down the wide river, with only the thick, unbroken jungle on each bank.

The Spaniards never found El Dorado, although the search went on for more than one hundred years. Many Spaniards died in the jungles and swamps of South America looking for "The Golden One."

ALONG THE RIVERS OF NORTH AMERICA

This painting shows Jacques Cartier's arrival in the new French colony in North America, on his third trip to the St. Lawrence. In the background are Native Americans shown wearing skins, and off to the right bears lurk in the woods.

While the Spaniards were searching for El Dorado in South America, the French, far to the north, were searching for their own kingdom of gold. From 1534 to 1541, the French explorer Jacques Cartier made three voyages to Canada's St. Lawrence River. He was delighted to discover what he thought were gold and diamonds. Unfortunately for Cartier, these turned out to be worthless iron pyrite (often called "fool's gold") and quartz crystals. The French were so disappointed that they did not return to Canada for fifty years.

In 1603, led by Samuel de Champlain, they sailed back to the St. Lawrence River. Champlain later founded the fort of Quebec and began to explore the surrounding land. He hoped to find a waterway to the Pacific, for trade with China. Like all the early explorers, he believed that the Pacific Ocean was only a short distance away. No one had any idea of the vastness of North America. The

Cartier sets off on his first journey up the St. Lawrence River. Cartier had been sent by the King of France to search for riches and for an easier route to the East.

French were challenged by the British, who settled on the East Coast and around Hudson Bay, to the north.

Vital assistance

The explorers would have gotten nowhere without the Native Americans' help. They showed the Europeans how to make canoes from birch bark. These could be used in most waters, were light enough to carry over "portages," and were easy to repair. They were the perfect craft for exploration.

All the explorers depended on Native American guides, who knew the rivers and the portages. They hunted and cooked for the explorers and paddled their canoes.

A Native American camp on Lake Huron. In the foreground are birch-bark canoes, which European travelers also used to travel up and down North American rivers.

The elusive ocean

The most famous journeys of exploration by canoe were made by a Scottish fur trader, Alexander Mackenzie. In 1789, he traveled down a river, now named after him, hoping it would lead to the Pacific.

A fur trapper in the Rocky mountains

Precious furs

The British and the French found that North America had its own source of wealth—the soft fur of the beaver, which was highly prized back in Europe. Many of the first explorers were traders and trappers. They began to push south and west, looking for new fur-trapping regions. Other explorers were missionaries, who wanted to convert the Native Americans to Christianity.

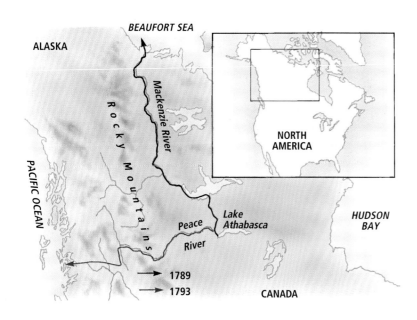

The routes of Alexander Mackenzie's two expeditions in search of an overland route across North America

But, unfortunately, it curved north toward the Arctic. Mackenzie named it the River of Disappointment.

In 1792–93, he made a second attempt to find a route to the Pacific, following the Peace River upstream to its source in the Rocky Mountains. There he hoped to find another river flowing west to the Pacific.

The Peace River had a strong current, and Mackenzie and his men had trouble rowing against it. In the foothills of the Rockies, they found continual rapids. They had to carry their canoes and their baggage up into the mountains.

Mackenzie hoped that the Rockies were a single wall of mountains, sloping down on the other side toward the Pacific. What he discovered was a series of mountain ranges, stretching as far as the eye could see.

He pushed onward through the snow, until he found a river, the Parsnip. He followed it to another river, the Fraser, that flowed toward the sea. After many difficulties,

Alexander Mackenzie is paddled up the Peace River, directed by a Native American guide.

16

Mackenzie reached the Pacific, becoming the first European to cross America north of Mexico. Now he had to go all the way home again.

Lewis and Clark

In 1803, President Thomas Jefferson organized an expedition to follow the course of the Missouri River. His hope was to find a waterway to the Pacific that could be used for trade.

In 1804, Meriwether Lewis and William Clark, leaders of the expedition, led a party of soldiers, hunters, and trappers from Kentucky to Canada. They were greatly helped by Sacajawea, a Native American guide, and her husband, Toussaint Charboneau. They were also joined by Baptiste Charboneau, Sacajawea's son to whom she gave birth during the journey.

Sacajawea— Lewis and Clark's guide— asks for directions from a group of Native Americans.

Toward understanding

One of the aims of the expedition was to win over the trust of the Native Americans and to learn as much as possible about them. Lewis and Clark recorded what they wore, what they ate, and what they believed in.

A people's tragedy

Lewis and Clark's reports described a way of life that was already vanishing. Vast numbers of Native Americans were dying of smallpox, brought to America by the Europeans. They described what they had learned of the history of the Mandan people: "The Mandans were settled 40 years ago in nine villages... seven on the west and two on the east side of the Missouri. The two, finding themselves wasting away before the smallpox...united into one village.... The same causes reduced the remaining seven.... They are now in two villages."

In 1837, a new wave of smallpox wiped the Mandan people out. Almost overnight, their numbers fell from 1,600 to 31.

Grizzly bears

Some of the most dangerous moments came from the fierce grizzly bears. An attempt to shoot a grizzly was described by Lewis: "They struck him several times...but the guns seemed only to direct the bear to them. In this manner he pursued two of them so close that they were obliged to throw aside their guns and pouches and throw themselves into the river. So enraged was this animal that he plunged into the river only a few feet behind the second man.... One of those who still remained on shore shot him through the head and killed him.... They found eight balls had passed through him in different directions."

The challenge of the Rockies

Like Mackenzie before them, Lewis and Clark were forced to climb into the vast Rocky Mountains. By September 1805, they were over a mile above sea level and heavy

The Buffalo Dance of the Mandan tribe. European explorers brought diseases that wiped out whole Native American tribes, including the Mandans.

snow was falling. Food was also running short, and the men lived on scraps of bear grease. They were saved by the Native Americans, who fed them dried salmon. Then, in October, they found the great Columbia River, which took them to the sea.

The explorers had no way of knowing the size of the Rocky Mountains. These stretch over three thousand miles, from northern Alaska down to New Mexico. In places they are hundreds of miles wide. Because of the Rockies, there is no practical water route to the Pacific. But Lewis and Clark had found a vast area, rich in beaver and salmon. They were soon followed by other explorers and settlers. For the Native Americans, this meant that their old way of life would vanish forever.

Below Lewis and Clark (center left) arrive at a Chinook Indian village on the Columbia River. Their Indian guide, Sacajawea, is using sign language to speak to the Chinooks.

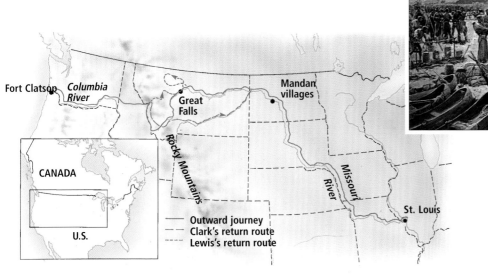

Left The route taken by Lewis and Clark from St. Louis to the Pacific and back again.

Fort Clatsop
Columbia River
Great Falls
Mandan villages
Rocky Mountains
Missouri River
CANADA
U.S.
St. Louis

—— Outward journey
– – Clark's return route
···· Lewis's return route

ACROSS THE DESERTS OF AUSTRALIA

British ships trading in the East in 1640. European and American traders spent centuries voyaging through the Spice Islands, never realizing that far to the south lay a continent—Australia.

Although Dutch explorers reached Australia in 1606, it was almost two hundred years before the first Europeans arrived to settle there. Many people were put off by the barren appearance of the continent and its distance from Europe. The first settlement, in 1788, was a British prison colony. The prisoners were followed by free settlers, who hoped to find a better life "down under."

The settlers brought many sheep and cattle with them. These animals were the great motive for the exploration of Australia—to find good grazing land.

Along the southern coast

The first settlements were scattered around the coast. There was Perth in the west, and Melbourne, Adelaide, and Sydney in the southeast. In 1840–41, Edward Eyre tried to find a route to take livestock between Adelaide and Perth. After failing to find an inland route, he decided to travel along the coast. He took one European, John Baxter, and three aborigines, as the Europeans called the native Australian people.

Eyre discovered the problem that would haunt all Australian explorers—lack of fresh water. Eyre survived by collecting dew from the bushes, a skill he learned from the aborigines.

Murder

By April, two of the aborigines were fed up. During the night of April 29, they killed John Baxter and fled. "The frightful, the appalling truth burst upon me that I was alone in the desert…. At the dead hour of the night, in the wildest and most inhospitable wastes of Australia…. I was left, with a single native…. I knew that not a drop of water or an ounce of flour had been left by these murderers…."

Saved!

Eyre and the one remaining aborigine, Wylie, staggered on. They were convinced that they had no chance of survival.

An aboriginal medicine man. European travelers across Australia could have learned how to survive from the aborigines, but instead they insisted on going it alone. Many explorers died as a result.

21

What saved them, on June 2, was the sight of a sail. It was a French whaler called the *Mississippi*: "Poor Wylie's joy knew no bounds, and he leapt and skipped about with delight as he congratulated me once more upon the prospect of getting plenty to eat."

The men lit a fire and hailed the vessel. Soon they were on board. Eyre wrote that it was a change "so great, so sudden, and so unexpected, that it seemed more like a dream than a reality."

Wylie and Eyre are attacked by aborigines. At first, aborigines offered to help newcomers to Australia, but soon they learned to try to fight them off. In the end, they were always unsuccessful against European weapons.

Into the outback

Eyre's terrible journey proved that there was no grazing land and very little water along the south coast. But perhaps there would be better luck in the center of Australia. All the other continents had lakes or inland seas and great rivers. It seemed only logical that Australia would also have them. This was the task of the explorers—to find a fertile region in the outback, as the inland area was called.

The search for an inland sea

In 1844, Charles Sturt set off north from the Darling River. He took with

Eyre rushes down the beach, into the arms of his rescuers. Close to death, he was lucky to be rescued by French whalers.

Excited townspeople turn out to watch the departure of Captain Sturt. He headed for the interior of Australia, convinced he would find an inland sea there.

him fifteen men, eleven horses, thirty bullocks, two hundred sheep, and a boat. Instead of reaching a sea, Sturt found himself in a burning desert. On January 27, 1845, he made camp at a creek where there was permanent water. The drought season was beginning, and Sturt could not risk moving forward or back. For seven months, the explorers stayed at the camp, watching the water level gradually sink in the creek, the plants die, and the birds fly away. Sturt wrote that his camp had become a "dreary prison: The tremendous heat... had parched vegetation and drawn moisture from everything.... Under its effects...our hair, as well as the wool on our sheep, ceased to grow, and our nails had become as brittle as glass...."

Europeans like Sturt found the outback a baffling place. Australian rivers did not behave like any rivers in Europe. A full river could turn into a dried-up creek in only a few weeks. The temperature also went through extreme changes. It was freezing cold at night and unbearably hot at midday.

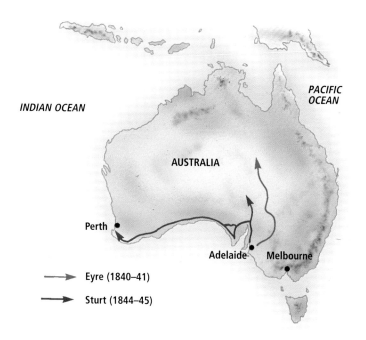

INDIAN OCEAN

PACIFIC OCEAN

AUSTRALIA

Perth

Adelaide Melbourne

→ Eyre (1840–41)
→ Sturt (1844–45)

Left The first towns and cities to be built in Australia were all dotted around the coast. Even as late as the mid-nineteenth century, the interior was unknown to all apart from the aborigines. Both Edward Eyre and Charles Sturt expected to find a vast inland sea in the middle of the continent, but instead they found only hot desert and salt flats.

Scurvy

By the beginning of March, Sturt was suffering from a disease which he described in his diary: "I had violent headaches, unusual pains in my joints, and a coppery taste in my mouth… it was only when my mouth became sore, and my gums spongy, that I felt it necessary to trouble Mr. Browne, who at once told me that I was laboring under an attack of scurvy, and I regretted to learn from him that both he and Mr. Poole were similarly afflicted."

Along with thirst and hunger, scurvy, caused by bad diet, was a common problem for Australian explorers. Two of Sturt's men died from it. At last, on July 11, the rain arrived, and Sturt was able to set off for home.

Well prepared… but ill advised

The best-equipped expedition of all was led by Robert O'Hara Burke, in 1860. His aim was to cross Australia from south to north and to find out what sort of territory lay inland.

Below Burke and Wills with their fellow travelers, ready to depart from Melbourne. In the foreground, mounted on one of his charges, is Mr. Landells, who was responsible for the camels. Behind him is the camel ambulance, for carrying sick explorers.

Burke, Wills, and Gray on their lone attempt to cross the Australian continent, accompanied by a pair of camels.

Burke had with him 18 men and plenty of supplies, carried by 28 horses and about 24 camels.

Burke, who had no knowledge of the outback, made a number of terrible mistakes. To travel faster, he dumped supplies, including his stock of lime juice. He did not realize that the juice, rich in vitamin C, was his best protection against scurvy. He made no attempt to make friends with the aborigines, the people who best understood how to survive in the desert. His second-in-command, William Wills, wrote: "Mr. Burke wants them to be kept at a safe distance at all times, and we ensure this by driving them off when they come too close."

Burke set up a base at a place called Cooper's Creek, and carried on with just three men—William Wills, Charley Gray, and John King. The rest, under William Brahe, were told to wait at the creek for more supplies from a relief party.

Robert O'Hara Burke, who died on the expedition at the age of 41

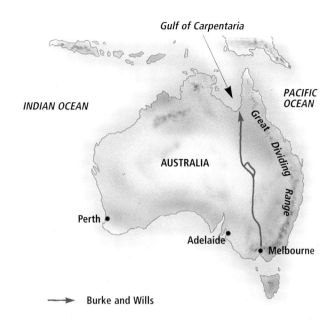

Gulf of Carpentaria

INDIAN OCEAN

PACIFIC OCEAN

AUSTRALIA

Great Dividing Range

Perth

Adelaide

Melbourne

→ Burke and Wills

The route of Burke and Wills's ill-fated expedition in 1860–61.

Traveling fast, Burke reached the north coast and then turned back. On the return journey, the rain poured continually and supplies ran low. By now they were suffering from scurvy. On April 17, Gray died, and the weakened men spent a whole day digging a grave for him.

They arrived back at Cooper's Creek to find that the others, also suffering from scurvy, had left just seven hours before. Brahe had left a note saying that the relief supplies had not arrived. Wills wrote: "We and our camels being just done up, and scarcely able to reach the depot, have very little chance of overtaking them…. Our disappointment at finding the depot deserted may easily be imagined."

After resting for two days, the men set off south down the creek, but found that it just led into the desert. While they were wandering, Brahe came back to look for them. But Burke had erased any signs that they had returned to Cooper's Creek. He didn't want the aborigines to follow them. Brahe left once more.

Returning to the creek, Burke, Wills, and King finally asked for help from the aborigines, who showed them how to grind and bake the seeds of a plant called nardoo. Despite this food, the men continued to weaken. On May 30, Wills wrote:

This fanciful picture shows the second of two search parties that were sent out to look for Burke and Wills.

Thin, worn-out and despairing, Burke and Wills lie near death. Once they had perished, their companion, King, was saved by aborigines, who fed him until he was rescued.

"We have been unable to leave the creek. Both camels are dead and our provisions are done…. We are trying to live the best way we can like the Blacks, but find it hard work. Our clothes are going to pieces fast."

Burke and Wills both died at the end of June 1861. King survived, thanks to the aborigines, who nursed him for a month until a search party found him. The explorers starved and died of thirst, despite all the equipment they carried. Yet the aborigines, who carried almost nothing, survived because they understood the outback.

INTO THE AFRICAN JUNGLE

Long before Europeans found out that America existed, they knew about Africa. Yet it was the last great continent that they explored. This was because travel in Africa was seen as difficult and dangerous, and the rewards of exploration seemed few.

Arab trade routes across the Sahara, linking the rich kingdoms of West Africa with Europe and the Middle East. The traders traveled across the desert, from one oasis to the next, in caravans of camels.

Muslim slavers

The Muslim Arabs, who conquered the north coast in the seventh century A.D., made a big contribution to the exploration of Africa. They set up trade routes across the Sahara, dealing in gold, copper, salt, ivory, cola nuts, and, above all, African slaves.

In the early nineteenth century, Arab slavers began to explore East Africa, from their base on the island of Zanzibar. This island became a holding place for vast numbers of slaves, who were then shipped off to markets in Arabia.

The slave market at Khartoum

An exhausted slave, unable to walk any further, is shot by the slaver.

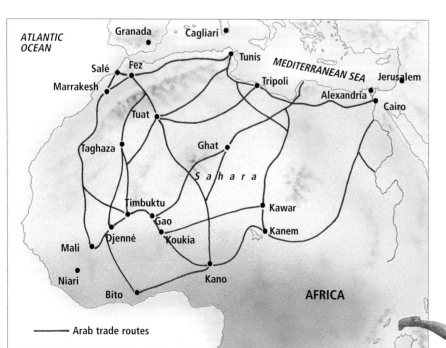

ATLANTIC OCEAN

Granada · Cagliari ·

Salé · Fez · Tunis
MEDITERRANEAN SEA
Marrakesh · Tripoli · Jerusalem
Alexandria · Cairo

Tuat

Taghaza · Ghat

S a h a r a

Timbuktu · Kawar
Gao
Djenné · Koukia · Kanem
Mali
Niari · Kano
Bito · **AFRICA**

—— Arab trade routes

Exploring for freedom

It was the wish to end the Muslim slave trade that drew many European explorers to Africa in the nineteenth century. One of the most famous was the Scottish missionary David Livingstone. He planned to end the slave trade by bringing Christianity to the heart of Africa and by opening up the country for trade with the outside world. Livingstone was a failure as a missionary. But he was a great traveler: in 1853–54, he covered almost five thousand miles, mainly on foot, as he crossed Africa from west to east.

African exploration involved tracing great rivers, like the Nile and the Congo, to their sources. In doing this, the explorers were solving age-old mysteries. They also felt thrilled to think that they were the first Europeans to see the African lakes and rivers.

A gentleman at all times

Henry Morton Stanley, a Welsh-born American, was the most successful explorer of Africa. He first went to Africa as a journalist, sent by *The New York Herald*. His job

Livingstone's canoe is attacked by a hippopotamus as he travels through the heart of Africa.

David Livingstone, the first great European explorer of Africa

Mauled by a lion

Africa was full of dangerous animals, including lions, crocodiles, hippos, elephants, rhinos, and snakes. Livingstone described being attacked by a lion in 1843: "Looking half round, I saw the lion just in the act of springing upon me... he caught my shoulder as he sprang, and we both came to the ground close together. Growling horribly close to my ear, he shook me as a terrier dog does a rat. The shock...caused a sort of dreaminess, in which there was no sense of pain nor feeling of terror."
The lion dropped Livingstone and turned on his followers, who were shooting at it. Livingstone survived, despite a crushed arm bone and eleven bite wounds.

was to find Livingstone, who had not been heard of for three years.

In November 1871, Stanley tracked Livingstone down, near Lake Tanganyika. He wrote: "I would have run to him, would have embraced him, only, he being an Englishman, I did not know how he would receive me; so I...walked deliberately to him, took off my hat, and said: 'Dr Livingstone, I presume?' 'Yes,' said he with a kind smile, lifting his cap slightly."

This meeting made Stanley world-famous and gave him a taste for more African exploration. Two years later, he set out to trace the Lualaba River, which

Henry Morton Stanley, the tough American journalist and traveler

flows out of Lake Victoria. He discovered that this river was the mighty Congo, which has its mouth in the Atlantic Ocean. He followed its entire course—a journey of almost three years.

Methods of travel

The problem with travel in Africa was that sleeping sickness, carried by the tsetse fly, killed horses, donkeys, and cattle. As a result, travel depended on human muscle. Stanley needed African helpers to carry his supplies and row his boats. He took with him an army of porters from Zanzibar, whom he treated very strictly.

To travel in Africa, Europeans needed vast amounts of supplies, including weapons, medicine, scientific equipment, tents, and cooking equipment. The bulk of their supplies was made up of trade goods, such as cloth and beads. These were swapped for food or given as presents to local chiefs. The chiefs always demanded gifts from strangers. If explorers refused, they would not be given food or water, and they might be attacked.

The preferred way of getting around in Africa—being carried in the shade by other people

In November 1871 Stanley finally found the most famous African explorer of all. He greeted him with the words: "Doctor Livingstone, I presume?" Livingstone, who had not seen another white man for over three years, replied simply, "Yes."

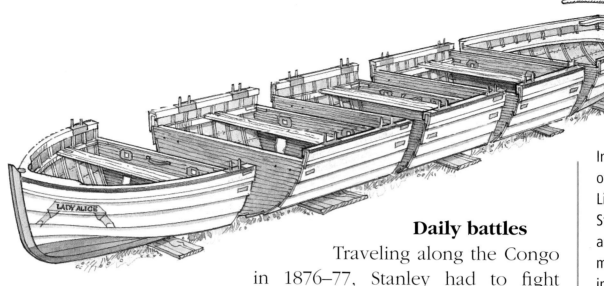

Stanley's 40-foot boat, *Lady Alice,* which was named after a fiancee who later jilted him. The boat was made in five sections and could be taken apart and carried around unnavigable stretches of river.

Daily battles

Traveling along the Congo in 1876–77, Stanley had to fight thirty-two battles. With his well-armed followers and his ruthless determination to succeed, he left a trail of slaughter behind him.

The African people saw the arrival of Stanley, with his army of porters, as an invasion. This is Stanley's description of the war canoes of the Soko people, at the beginning of his twenty-eighth battle: "Down the natives came, fast and furious, but in magnificent style… their canoes were enormous things, one especially, a monster of 80 paddlers…. The chiefs pranced up and down a planking that ran from stern to stern. On a platform near the bow were choice fellows swaying their long spears at the ready."

In over 35 years of exploration, Livingstone and Stanley visited and mapped much of the interior of southern Africa. While mapping the continent's rivers, Livingstone traveled almost 31,000 miles, mostly on foot.

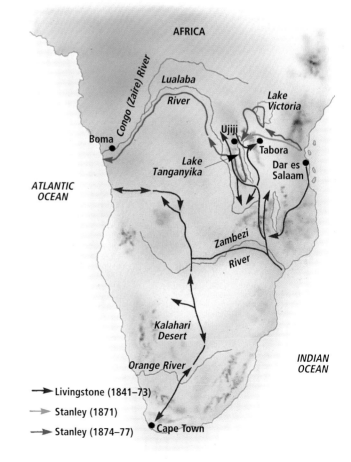

AFRICA

Congo (Zaire) River

Lualaba River

Boma

Lake Victoria

Ujiji

Tabora

Lake Tanganyika

Dar es Salaam

ATLANTIC OCEAN

Zambezi River

Kalahari Desert

Orange River

INDIAN OCEAN

Cape Town

→ Livingstone (1841–73)
→ Stanley (1871)
→ Stanley (1874–77)

Armed with rifles, Stanley's men were much more deadly. The Soko were soon fleeing from the bloodstained river. Stanley chased them and set fire to their village.

Right Stanley and his men hack their way through the jungle, hauling his boat behind them, on his 1874–77 expedition to Lakes Victoria and Tanganyika and the Congo. In the background lurk African tribesmen, with whom Stanley fought many fierce battles.

"The virtue of a good whip"

Stanley's success came from his physical toughness, his energy, and his ruthlessness. He whipped his porters to drive them on and refused to stop for rests. Describing his first expedition, he wrote, "The virtue of a good whip was well tested by me on this day."

Spirits, monsters, and men in boxes

When the Africans saw European explorers for the first time, they were usually amazed or terrified by the sight of white skin. Winwood Reade, who visited West Africa in the 1850s, described this attitude: "Here stood two men, with their hands upon each other's shoulders, staring at me in mute wonder, their eyes like saucers… a man was dragging up his frightened wife to look at me and a child cried bitterly with averted eyes."

A common belief was that white people were spirits or ghosts, or that they lived beneath the sea, because they often arrived by boat. One African name for a white person was muzungu, or "sea monster." White people were also believed to be cannibals. They were thought to have amazing magical powers. Some porters thought that the boxes they carried held spare, fold-up white men, which could be put together in an emergency.

Africans could never understand why the white people had come. In 1863, the explorer Samuel Baker was searching for one of the sources of the Nile. The local people, the Nyoro, remembered his visit in stories, which were later written down. Here is how they described the meeting of Baker, nick-named "the Beard," with

Livingstone, on his last African journey, finally succumbed to disease. Tired and ill, he died in 1873, near the shores of Lake Bangweulu in what is now Zambia.

Disease

The biggest cause of death among the explorers was disease. They all suffered from malaria, and many died from it. Other diseases included sleeping sickness, dysentery, worms, river blindness, and yellow fever.

A nineteenth-century medical book warned British travelers in Africa to expect "shivering, lassitude (tiredness), headache and backache… raving delirium…vomiting of blood."

their chief, Kamurasi: "The Beard explained to him that... they had taken this very long journey out from England to look for a large lake which his friends had heard lay somewhere near.... Then Kamurasi knew that the stranger was speaking lies, for no man would leave his own country and people, and face danger and fatigue, merely to look at water."

Samuel Baker and his wife, Florence, with John Hanning Speke and James Grant, who were searching for the source of the Nile River.

THE RACE TO THE SOUTH POLE

Right Elephant Island, in Antarctica. With a temperature rarely above freezing, howling winds, and constant darkness for months on end, this is the most hostile environment on Earth.

The most hostile place on our planet is Antarctica, the frozen land around the South Pole. Antarctica is covered by a huge, slowly moving sheet of ice, which also sticks out over the sea to form huge floating shelves.

Travel in the Antarctic is very difficult. The freezing cold causes frostbite, damage to the skin and flesh that is similar to burns. The glare of sunlight reflecting off the snow can cause temporary blindness. There is the risk of tumbling into deep crevasses, hidden by thin bridges of snow. Sudden blizzards can make all movement impossible. Yet another problem is that the Pole itself is on a high plateau, nearly one thousand feet above sea level where the air is thin. This makes all physical effort very difficult. It is not surprising that this was the last continent on Earth to be explored.

First attempts

In 1901, three British explorers, Robert Falcon Scott, Ernest Shackleton, and Edward Wilson, made the first attempt to reach the South Pole, by sledding across the vast ice shelf. They took dogs with them to pull the sleds, but they had constant trouble with them. This was because they did not understand how to use the dogs. However, Scott decided that it was the fault of the animals. Weakened by cold and scurvy, the expedition was forced to turn back, 540 miles from its goal.

Shackleton made a second attempt in 1908. He discovered the huge Beardmore Glacier and climbed it to the Polar Plateau. But after reaching a point only 97 miles from the Pole, he was again forced to turn back.

In 1909, Scott announced that he was returning to the Antarctic. The Pole was not supposed to be the main purpose of the expedition. Its aim was scientific research.

Ernest Shackleton at his camp on Cape Royds. His clothing is remarkably unsuitable for the Antarctic, showing how unprepared early explorers were for the land they visited.

Why would anybody want to go there?

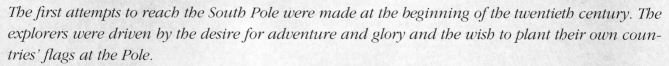

The first attempts to reach the South Pole were made at the beginning of the twentieth century. The explorers were driven by the desire for adventure and glory and the wish to plant their own countries' flags at the Pole.

As the last unknown continent on earth, Antarctica also had great scientific interest. Scientists wanted to study its wildlife, including penguins and seals, its rocks, and its weather patterns.

But it was the Pole that captured people's imaginations. More than 8,000 men applied to join the expedition, mainly from the British navy or army. Scott chose 65 men, including a scientific staff of 12. Very few of them had any experience of polar exploration.

Rivals for glory

Scott had a rival, a Norwegian explorer named Roald Amundsen. He originally planned to go to the North Pole, not the South. In 1907, he raised money and borrowed a ship, the *Fram* ("Forward"), from an older explorer, Fridtjof Nansen. His plans changed when he heard that two separate American explorers, Robert Peary and Frederick Cook, had each reached the North Pole. Amundsen later wrote: "If the expedition was to be saved, I had to act quickly and without hesitation. I decided on a change of front—to turn about and point my bows south."

Amundsen kept his change of plans secret until he was safely at sea. He worried that his government, anxious not to upset the British, would not let him go to the South Pole.

The *Fram*, which the determined Norwegian explorer Roald Amundsen took to the Antarctic, having promised its owner that he was going only to the North Pole.

Robert Falcon Scott of the Royal Navy. Scott was determined that he would be the first man to the South Pole. The calendar this picture was printed with said that his efforts "exercised a high moral influence on the hearts and consciences of men."

Very different preparations

"Victory awaits him who has everything in order. Defeat is certain for him who has neglected to take the necessary precautions."
—Roald Amundsen

Amundsen recruited 19 men, all chosen for their skill and experience. Unlike Scott's men, they were expert skiers and dog-drivers. Amundsen prepared with great care. He had studied the methods of travel used by the Inuit, the native people of the Arctic. To pull his sleds, he bought the toughest Inuit dogs from the north of Greenland. He had special snow goggles made, based on the slitted ones worn by the Inuit but with glass filters added. He designed his own sled cases with circular openings—unlike the usual cases, these could be opened and closed on the sled without having to untie ropes. Anything that could save energy would help the expedition.

In contrast Scott's preparations were rushed. Much of his equipment was badly designed. His woolen and canvas clothing was twice the weight of Amundsen's Inuit furs and not as warm or waterproof. His small, round goggles misted up easily and gave poor protection against snow blindness.

Scott's biggest mistake was to take ponies, which were unsuited to the Antarctic. They could not stand the cold. With their heavy bodies and sharp hooves, they tumbled into crevasses. Their food of hay and grass did not grow there, so it all had to be brought along. In contrast, Amundsen's dogs could be fed on seals, penguins, and one another.

Above Amundsen dressed in Inuit furs, ready for almost anything the polar weather could throw at him.

Left Scott's clothes, in contrast to Amundsen's, were flimsy, too heavy, and inadequate.

Roald Amundsen, with one of the dog teams that his expedition to the Pole was to use with great success

Dog power

On October 19, 1911, Amundsen set off with four men and four light sleds, each pulled by thirteen dogs. The men skied while the dogs raced forward, pulling the lightly loaded sleds.

Part of Amundsen's plan was to kill half of his dogs halfway to the Pole, to provide fresh meat for the men and the rest of the dogs. He described the killing: "Twenty-four of our brave and faithful companions were marked out for death. We had agreed

Scott—sentimental about having to shoot them—had shrunk from taking dogs all the way to the Pole. He took ponies instead (shown here on his ship, the *Terra Nova*), and in the end had to shoot his "trusty servants" anyway.

to shrink from nothing in order to reach our goal. Shot now followed upon shot—they had an uncanny sound over the great plain. A trusty servant lost his life each time. In everybody's view, there was no other way." The men pressed on with three sleds.

There were setbacks, such as a blinding storm that held them up for four days. One area, which they called the Devil's Dance-Floor, had a surface of thin ice with many hidden crevasses—the dogs pulling one of the sleds disappeared into a crevasse and had to be dragged up again.

Human power

At the beginning of November 1911, Scott set off with motor-driven sleds, ponies, and dogs. The motor sleds broke down. The ponies got stuck in the snow and had to be shot. Only the dogs were successful, but Scott had already decided to send them back at the foot of the Beardmore Glacier.

One of the lightweight, Inuit-style sleds that sped Amundsen and his men to the South Pole.

The Norwegians at the Pole. They reached it and raised the flag on December 14, 1911. The race was only half-run—they still had to get home. At this point, Scott's party was still laboring on foot across the ice.

He hated the cruelty of whipping dogs and of killing them to feed one another.

Scott had decided to use human-haulage for the last part of the journey. In his earlier book, *The Voyage of the Discovery*, he had explained why this was the best way to travel: "No journey ever made with dogs can approach the height of that fine conception… when a party of men go forth to face hardships, dangers, and difficulties with their own unaided efforts…. Surely in this case the conquest is more nobly and splendidly won."

For the last part of the journey, Scott and his team of four men had to pull a single, heavily loaded sled. Dragging it across the Polar Plateau was a hard, slow business.

A terrible shock

"The worst has happened… We found sled tracks and ski tracks going and coming and the clear trace of dogs' paws—many dogs. This told us the whole story. The Norwegians have forestalled us and are first at the Pole. It is a terrible disappointment…. All the daydreams must go."
Scott's diary, January 16, 1912

A dog-team similar to the one used in Scott's doomed race for the Pole.

First to the Pole

On December 14, 1911, Amundsen reached the Pole. He later recalled: "The goal was reached, the journey ended…. We proceeded to the greatest and most solemn act of the whole journey—the planting of our flag. Pride and affection shone in the five pairs of eyes that gazed upon the flag, as it unfurled itself with a sharp crack, and waved over the Pole."

Scott, Oates, Evans, Bowers, and Wilson at the South Pole, January 17, 1912, over a month after the Norwegians. Disappointed and exhausted, they never saw their friends and families again, but died in the snow and ice.

Scott at the Pole

The mood of the British expedition was very different. On January 17, 1912, they found the Norwegian flag flying at the Pole. Scott wrote: "Great God! This is an awful place…. Now for a run home and a desperate struggle."

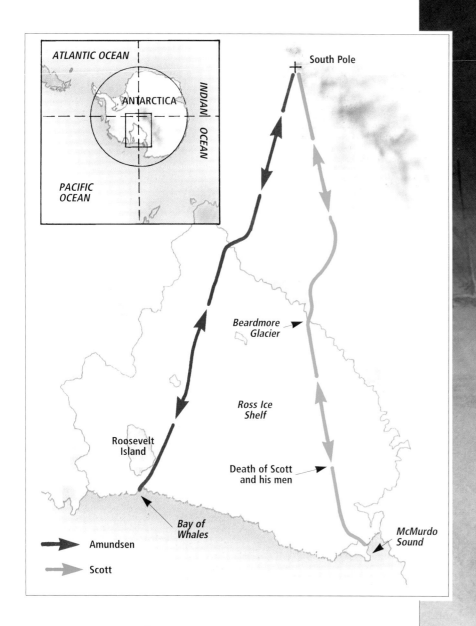

The routes of Amundsen and Scott. Even before the final dash for the Pole began, Amundsen was 60 miles closer than Scott to their goal.

Captain Oates stumbles away from the camp on the ice. He could barely walk and is supposed to have left his companions with the words, "I may be some time." He died hoping that they would have a better chance of survival without him holding them up.

The men were suffering from frostbite and hunger. Evans, the biggest of them, suffered most from hunger and was the first to die. Then Lawrence Oates, who could barely walk, struggled out of the tent into the night. He knew that the others would have a better chance without him. They died later, starving and freezing, trapped in their tent by a blizzard. Their frozen bodies were found eight months later by a search party.

With the success of the Amundsen expedition, the last continent had been visited by human beings. Many considered the great age of exploration to be over. But with the advances of technology came new challenges—flight, undersea travel, and space travel—which ensure the possibility of great journeys for a long time to come.

TIME LINE

A.D. 1350 **1600** **1850**

106 B.C.
The Silk Road, linking China and the west, first used

629–45
Hsüan-tsang travels from China to India and back

1213
Mongols begin their conquests

1246
Giovanni de Pian del Carpini travels to the Mongol court

1275–92
Marco Polo in China

1325–49
Ibn Battuta of Tangiers travels all over the known Muslim world

1492
Christopher Columbus crosses the Atlantic and begins conquest of the Americas

1519–21
Spaniards conquer the Aztec Empire of Mexico

1531–35
Spaniards conquer the Inca Empire of Peru

1534–41
Jacques Cartier explores the St. Lawrence River, Canada

1541
Francisco de Orellana travels 1,000 miles down the Amazon River

1608
Samuel de Champlain founds Quebec in Canada

1788
First European settlement in Australia, a British prison colony at Botany Bay

1792–93
Alexander Mackenzie crosses North America to the Pacific Ocean

1804–06
Lewis and Clark lead expedition across North America from St. Louis to the Pacific

1840–41
Edward Eyre explores the south coast of Australia

1844
Charles Sturt fails to find an inland sea in Australia

1853–56
David Livingstone travels across Africa and sees the Victoria Falls

1860–61
Burke and Wills cross Australia

1876–77
Henry Stanley travels down the Congo River in Africa

1901–04
Robert Falcon Scott's first attempt to reach the South Pole

1910–12
Roald Amundsen and Scott each lead expeditions to the South Pole. Amundsen gets there first, on December 14, 1911. Scott's men all die on the return journey.

GLOSSARY

Aborigines A name given to the native people of Australia. It means, simply, people who were there "from the beginning."

Buddhist A follower of the religion started in the sixth century B.C. by the Indian prince, Siddhartha Gautama, the Buddha, or enlightened one.

Cannibals People who eat human flesh.

Crevasse A deep split in an ice sheet, often hidden by surface snow.

Dysentery Severe diarrhea, including the passing of blood, caused by the infection of the intestine by bacteria.

Fever Raised body heat as a symptom of an illness.

Glacier A mass of ice moving slowly downhill, often found in mountain valleys.

Malaria A disease, carried by female mosquitoes, which is common in hot, marshy places.

Muslims Followers of Islam, the religion founded in Arabia in the early seventh century A.D. by Muhammad.

Outback The name given to the remote inland areas of Australia.

Pilgrimage A journey for religious reasons to a holy place.

Plateau A wide, flat area of high land.

Portage Carrying a boat overland from one waterway to another, especially in North America. The name also refers to the land routes between the waterways.

River blindness A disease caused by a parasitic worm. Victims may lose their sight.

Scurvy A disease caused by lack of vitamin C (found in fresh vegetables and fruit).

Silk Road The name given to the overland trade route between China and the west, first opened up in 106 B.C.

Sleeping sickness A disease found in Central Africa, caused by the blood-sucking tsetse fly.

Smallpox A disease caused by a virus, which European explorers carried with them to the Americas.

FURTHER READING

Arnold, Nick. *Voyages of Exploration.* Remarkable World. New York: Thomson Learning, 1995.

Chrisp, Peter. *The Search for a Northern Route.* Exploration and Encounters. New York: Thomson Learning, 1993.

Duggleby, John. *Doomed Expeditions.* Incredible Histories. New York: Crestwood House, 1990.

Grant, Neil. *The Great Atlas of Discovery.* New York: Alfred A. Knopf Books for Young Readers, 1992.

Matthews, Rupert. *Explorer.* New York: Alfred A. Knopf Books for Young Readers, 1992.

Rozakis, Laurie, *Henson & Peary: The Race for the North Pole.* Partners. Woodbridge, CT: Blackbirch Press, 1994.

Sherman, Steven. *Henry Stanley and the European Explorers of Africa.* World Explorers. New York: Chelsea House, 1993.

Strathern, Paul. *Exploration by Land.* Silk and Spice Routes. New York: New Discovery, 1994.

Twist, Clint. *Lewis and Clark: Exploring the Northwest.* Beyond the Horizons. Milwaukee: Raintree Steck-Vaughn, 1994.

Twist, Clint. *Marco Polo: Overland to Medieval China.* Beyond the Horizons. Milwaukee: Raintree Steck-Vaughn, 1994.

INDEX